Copy Cat

For Emma Nash,

who loves to draw.

A.P.

First published in 2016 by Nosy Crow Ltd
The Crow's Nest, 10a Lant Street
London SE1 1QR
www.nosycrow.com

ISBN 978 0 85763 681 2 (HB)
ISBN 978 0 85763 682 9 (PB)

Nosy Crow and associated logos are trademarks
and/or registered trademarks of Nosy Crow Ltd.

A CIP catalogue record for this book is available from the British Library.

Printed in China by Imago

Papers used by Nosy Crow are made from wood grown in sustainable forests.

1 3 5 7 9 8 6 4 2 (HB)
1 3 5 7 9 8 6 4 2 (PB)

Copy Cat

Ali Pye

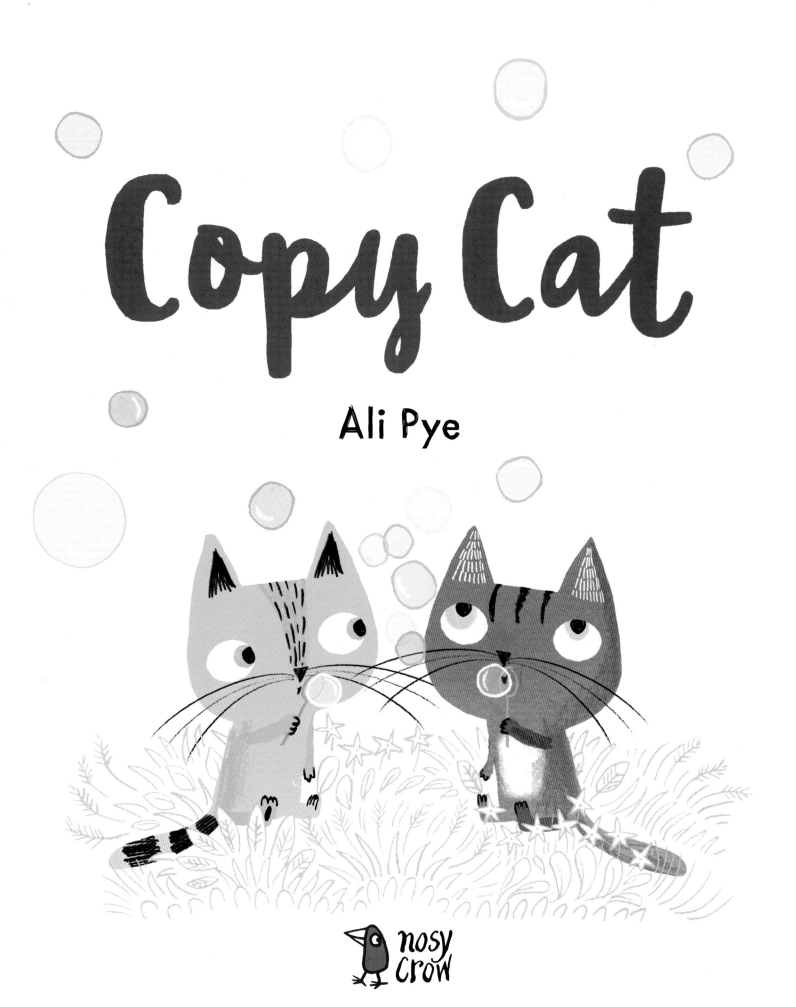

nosy crow

Bella loved Anna.

In fact, Bella loved Anna **so much**
that she wanted to be **just** like her.

When Anna played hula-hoop . . .

. . . Bella wanted to play hula-hoop too,
just like Anna.

When Anna played ballerinas . . .

And when Anna played pirates . . .

. . . Bella wanted to be a ballerina too,
just like Anna.

. . . Bella wanted to play pirates too,
just like Anna.

So, when Anna played princesses . . .

. . . well, of course, Bella wanted to be a princess too, **just** like Anna . . .

. . . except there was only
one crown!

Anna was **cross**.

"Bella!" she said.
"You are such a copycat!
Stop copying me!
I'm the princess. And it's my crown!"

And off Anna went, all huffy-puffy,
to play princesses by herself.

'What am I going to do now?'
thought Bella.

There was **no one** to play with,
no one to copy.
She'd have to play by herself, too.

After a while, Bella got a skipping rope
out of the toy box. She didn't know how to
skip and, at first, she got all tangled up.
But she unwound herself and then
she **practised**
and **practised**
and **practised** . . .

. . . until she was skipping
so fast she didn't notice that
Chloe was watching.

"You're a good skipper, Bella," said Chloe. "I wish I could do that, too."

"It's easy!" said Bella. "Just **copy** me!"

So they found a rope for Chloe, and Bella slowed
down a bit so that Chloe could copy her.
And Chloe **practised**

and **practised**

and **practised** . . .

. . . until she could skip too, **just** like Bella.

While Bella and Chloe were skipping . . .

. . . Anna was being a huffy-puffy
princess all by herself.

It was **no fun**
at all.

So she went to find Bella.

But she found Bella **and** Chloe,
skipping away like anything.

"You're **such** good skippers," said Anna, forgetting
to be huffy-puffy. "I wish I could do that, too."

"It's easy!" said Bella and Chloe. "Just **copy** us!"
So they found a rope for Anna, and they slowed
down so she could copy them.

Anna **practised** and **practised** and **practised**
until she could skip **just** like Bella and Chloe.
Then Chloe had a brilliant idea.

They found a big long rope.

And they **all** skipped . . . **together.**

Then they all played hula-hooping-
ballerina-pirate-princesses . . .

. . . together.

Sometimes they liked to copy each other . . .

. . . but sometimes they
didn't copy anyone at all.

Well, no one **except** . . .

. . . DOTTY!